POLLY $^{AND}_{THE}$ PUFFIN

Windsor and Maidenhead

38067170013998

KT-380-490

15

Jenny
COLGAN

POLLY AND THE PUFFIN

LB

LITTLE, BROWN BOOKS FOR YOUNG READERS

First published in Great Britain in 2015
by Little, Brown Books for Young Readers

Copyright © Jenny Colgan 2015
Illustrations © Thomas Docherty 2015 (based on characters originated by Jenny Colgan)

The moral rights of Jenny Colgan and Thomas Docherty to be identified
as author and illustrator respectively have been asserted.

All characters and events in this publication, other than those
clearly in the public domain, are fictitious and any resemblance
to real persons, living or dead, is purely coincidental.

All rights reserved.
No part of this publication may be reproduced, stored in a retrieval system,
or transmitted, in any form or by any means, without the prior permission
in writing of the publisher, nor be otherwise circulated in any form of binding
or cover other than that in which it is published and without a similar condition
including this condition being imposed on the subsequent purchaser.

A CIP catalogue record for this book
is available from the British Library.

ISBN 978-0-349-13190-0

3 5 7 9 10 8 6 4 2

Printed in Italy

Papers used by LBYR are from well-managed forests and other responsible sources.

Little, Brown Books for Young Readers,
an imprint of Hachette Children's Group and published by Hodder and Stoughton Limited
338 Euston Road, London NW1 3BH

www.hachette.co.uk

www.lbkids.co.uk

For D, who has been waiting for this.

The storm howled outside the little house by the sea, but Polly was safe and warm in her bed. Then . . .

What was that?
Polly crept bravely –

creepity creepity

– down the dark steps
and through the dark door,
and into the dark kitchen . . .

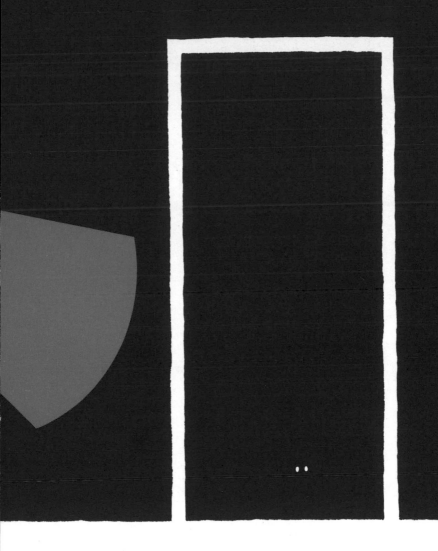

where she thought she might see . . .

A MONSTER?

NO!
It was not a monster.

A HUGE SPIDER FROM OUTER SPACE?

NO!

It was not a huge spider
from outer space (phew).

It was a bird. A little bird who had crashed in the storm –

CRASH!

– right through the front door and onto the floor.

Polly and the bird looked at one another.

It was a puffin. He had big black eyes and a big orange beak.

"Hello," said Polly.

"Eep," said the puffin. His wing hung stiffly at his side.

Polly's mummy went to find the First Aid box. Together, they put a bandage on his wing.

"Are you hungry?" Polly asked,
crouching to peer into the puffin's big,
black eyes.

"Eep," said the puffin.

They gave him some tuna fish.

He liked it.

They gave him a sandwich.

He liked it.

Polly wanted to give him some of her
lollipop, but Polly's mummy said no.

"I think I shall call you 'Neil'," Polly said.
"Eep!" said Neil.

They took Neil to see the vet.

"You're doing a good job of looking after him," the vet said, smiling. "He's a very healthy puffling. His wing will get better quickly."

"What's a puffling?" Polly asked.

"That's the name for baby puffins," her mummy told her.

"Now, Polly," said the vet. "Do you think you can look after this puffin until his wing is all better?"

"Yes," said Polly.

"Once he can fly again, you will have to let him go back to join his puffin friends," the vet told her.

Polly was not sure about this one little bit. She wanted Neil to stay for ever.

Every day, Neil grew
a little better.

He hopped.

He fluttered.

He swam in the
cooking pot.

He played
in the sink.

He fought with
the watering can.

He slept in a box.

27

He ate EVERYTHING.

And at night, before they went
to sleep, he would let Polly ruffle the
feathers on the back of his neck.

"I love my puffin," Polly said.

"You know," said Polly's mummy.
"He's not really your puffin. Puffins don't
belong to anyone. They live wild by the sea."

"We live wild by the sea," said Polly.

"I do my best," her mummy said.

One day Polly came home from school and looked around. "Where's Neil?" she asked.

Her mummy took her outside. Neil was sitting on the windowsill of Polly's bedroom. His claws clung to the edge. "What's he doing?" said Polly.

"I'm not sure," said her mummy. "But I think he wants to fly."

Polly stretched up on her tiptoes.
"Come on, Neil. You can fly!"
"Eep!" said Neil in a scared voice.

"Maybe he'll fly down for a bit of my bun," said Polly. "He loves buns."

She ran to the kitchen and came back, holding out a bun with pink icing. Neil stepped closer to the edge of the sill.

Her mummy put her hands up ready
to catch him as Neil took one step . . .
two steps . . . and woohoo! He flittered
and fluttered and flapped – Neil was
flying!

He circled the little house by the sea.

"Neil can fly!" said Polly, clapping. "My puffin can fly. You're the best puffin ever, Neil!"

Her mummy put an arm around Polly's shoulders.

"Yes," she said. "He's all better. Now, we'll have to let him go back and find his mummy and his friends."

"I forgot that. Can't I be his mummy?"
said Polly.

Neil landed on the ground and
pecked the last of the bun. Polly rubbed
the back of his head.

"You have been a very good mummy, but all pufflings grow up and fly away," her mummy said gently.

"What if they don't want to fly away?" Polly asked. Maybe her mummy was wrong. Maybe Neil didn't want to leave them at all.

Neil flapped his wings and took off
again, flying around in the sky above
them. They watched him head towards
the stormy sea and turn above the waves
before he came back.

"They always do, my darling," her
mummy said.

Polly looked up at her. "I will never
want to fly away from you," she said to
her mummy.

Her mummy gave her a big cuddle,
just like this one I am giving you now.

It was time to let Neil go. Polly and her mummy went to a special place with lots and lots of puffins for Neil to play with. It was called a 'sanctuary'. A nice lady put a little blue strap around Neil's ankle so they would always be able to recognise Neil when they came back to visit.

Polly knew she'd be able to recognise him anyway, but she was very polite and didn't mention it.

Polly kissed Neil on the beak and scratched the back of his head one last time.

"I will miss you, Neil," she said.

"Eep," said Neil.

Then he took

one step . . .   two steps . . .   three steps . . .

and then,

WOO HOO!

He flapped his wings and flew off into the sky. He joined all the other puffins who were flying high, chattering, playing together.

Polly and her mummy watched as the birds whirled round and round. The puffins flew further and further out across the waves, until Neil disappeared.

Polly felt sad. Her mummy bought
her a toy puffin to play with, but it wasn't
the same.

"I don't like this Wrong Puffin,"
she said.

"But he will help you always remember Neil and how you made him better," said her mummy. "And that is a very important thing."

Polly wasn't sure about that.

Polly sat at the window looking for Neil. She sat looking on stormy days.

She sat looking on sunny days.

She sat looking on snowy days.

Sometimes she held Wrong Puffin.
But all she saw was the sea and the
clouds and the lighthouse. She couldn't
see Neil anywhere.

Then, one
morning, Polly
woke up and found
something on her window
sill.

It was a long black feather.
She ran downstairs.

"I think Neil left me a present!"
she said.

"Maybe," said her mummy.

Polly's mummy took her outside.
There on the ground in front of the little
house by the sea was another feather . . .

and on the harbour wall there was
another one . . .

and on the rocks by the lighthouse was
another one.

They followed the trail and climb,
climb, climbed the old stone steps of
the lighthouse rock with the shells
beside it.

At the very top rock they found . . .

NEiL!!!!

Not just Neil. There was another
puffin next to him. They had a cosy nest
in the rocks, and beneath them Polly
spotted a glimpse of white.

It was . . .

an egg!

"NEIL!" shouted Polly, dropping Wrong Puffin.

Neil left his friend and waddled over to let Polly scratch the back of his head.

"You know, you must never touch a bird's eggs," Polly's mummy said, though Polly knew this already.

"He wanted us to visit him, didn't
he?" she asked, slipping her hand into
her mummy's.

Together, they gazed at the two
puffins.

"Yes," her mummy said. "I think
you're right. I think he really did."

That night, Polly's mummy tucked her in
with Wrong Puffin and the feather.

She felt all safe and warm and happy
in her bed.

She could hear the wind beyond her
bedroom, singing around the house.
She imagined the storm racing over
the cliffs, out to sea where . . .

The puffins dance –

WOO

RECIPES

Polly and her mummy love baking
and Neil loves eating the results.
If you want to have your own fun
in the kitchen, here are two recipes
that you can make with a grown-up.

Puffins!

Puffins are a mixture of pancakes and muffins and are very easy and delicious!
First, ask your grown-up to turn the oven on to 180 degrees C.
Grease a muffin pan. Smaller is better, as these bakes don't rise very high.
Then make your puffin mix!

INGREDIENTS

- 200 grams (7 ounces) self raising flour

- 3 eggs

- 400 mls milk

- 1 tablespoon olive oil

- Pinch salt

- 1 tablespoon baking powder

INSTRUCTIONS

1. Place all the ingredients in a large bowl. Whisk them together.

2. Pour the mixture into a greased muffin tray.

3. Now, you can get creative with your toppings! Lemon? Hazelnut? Chocolate chips? Cinnamon? Blueberries? It's completely up to you. If you put blueberries in, your puffins will all turn blue.

4. Place your tray in the oven and bake for 10 minutes, or until golden brown on top.

5. Turn out your puffins onto a cooling tray and leave to cool.

6. Add a dipping sauce – maple syrup, crème fraiche and honey are all good.

7. Dip and munch!

PUFFINS CAN LIVE FOR UP TO 35 YEARS.

Polly's Buns

These are buns that Polly bakes. Neil loves the pink icing. You can make some, too!

INGREDIENTS

- 50 grams (1.7 ounces) caster sugar

- 50 grams (1.7 ounces) butter

- 150ml milk

- 1 sachet of dried yeast

- 400 grams (14 ounces) plain white flour

- Pinch salt

- 1 large egg, beaten

- If you would like a fruit bun, add 125 grams (4.4 ounces) raisins to the mix.

PUFFINS MATE FOR LIFE, CHOOSING A PARTNER WHEN THEY ARE BETWEEN THREE AND FIVE YEARS OLD.

INSTRUCTIONS

1. Put sugar, butter and milk in a small saucepan.

2. Ask a grown-up to heat the mixture very gently until just warm. Don't let it get too hot.

3. Pour the mixture into a bowl and mix in the yeast.

4. Leave for 10 minutes. The mixture should get a little bit foamy.

5. Whisk the egg, mix it in to the wet mixture.

6. Sift the flour into a large bowl and add salt.

7. Pour the wet mix into a well in a centre of the flour.

8. Use a metal spoon and then your hands to make this into a ball, and place on a floured surface.

9 Knead the mixture – this means hit and punch it about a bit! – for about five minutes, or until the mix is nice and smooth.

10 Place it back in the bowl, cover with a clean teatowel and leave it somewhere warm for an hour and a half to rise.

11 Divide the mixture into eight small circles, and place them on a large baking tray covered in baking paper. You can flatten them down a little bit.

PUFFINS ARE INCREDIBLE FLIERS AND SWIMMERS. THEY CAN DIVE DOWN AS FAR AS 60 METRES TO CATCH FISH! AND THEY CAN FLY AT 88 MPH!

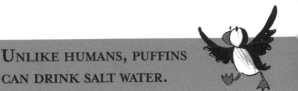

12 Leave for another 45 minutes, then bake at 190 degrees C for 20 minutes, or until golden brown.

13 Remove from the oven and put the buns on a cooling tray to cool.

You can slice your buns open and fill with jam or honey. Polly likes to make pink icing by mixing up some icing sugar with a little water and a couple of drops of red food colouring. The buns must be cool before icing, otherwise pink icing will run everywhere. Then eat straight away!

JOKES

Q: Which bird is always out of breath?

A: A puffin!

Q: Which fish can perform operations?

A: A sturgeon!

Q: What do you call a man with a puffin nesting on his head?

A: Cliff!

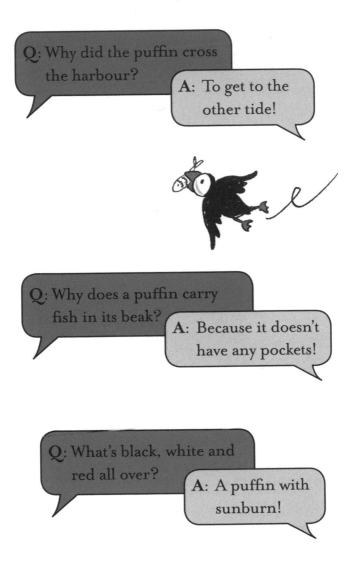

Q: What is black and white, black and white, black and white?

A: A puffin rolling down a hill!

Knock knock.

Who's there?

Neil.

Neil who?

Kneel down and give me a cuddle!

Q: Why do puffins fly south in the winter?

A: Because it's too far to walk!

Q: What do sea monsters eat?

A: Fish and ships!

Q: Why are dolphins so clever?

A: Because they swim in schools!

Q: What fish can you see at night?

A: A starfish!

Q: Why did the flounder go to see the doctor?

A: Because he was feeling a bit flat!

Q: Where do puffins go for a coffee?

A: To the nest-café!

Q: Which bird can dance better than a puffin?

A: The pelican-can!

Q: Why don't oysters share their pearls?

A: Because they're shellfish!

Q: What is the strongest creature in the sea?

A: A mussel!

Q: What is a puffin's favourite TV show?

A: The feather forecast!

Q: What is an eel's favourite dance?

A: The conger!

Q: What do you call a fish with no eyes?

A: Fsh!

Q: What did the sea say to the puffin?

A: Nothing, it just waved!

Q: What is yellow and dangerous?

A: Shark-infested custard!

Q: When should you buy a puffin?

A: When it's going cheeeeep!

ACTIVITIES

How to make fat cakes for birds

Birds need to eat fat, especially in winter, to help keep them warm and healthy. This is a recipe to make fat cakes which you can hang in your garden or outside your window, and then watch to see which birds come and feed. You never know, it might tempt a hungry puffin...

PUFFIN FEATHERS ARE COATED IN AN OILY SUBSTANCE THAT KEEPS THEM WARM IN FREEZING WATER.

Please note – *although these are called cakes, we don't recommend eating them if you're not a bird! They wouldn't hurt you but would taste pretty yucky and make you feel sick.*

YOU WILL NEED:

- Old yoghurt pots
- String or twine
- Lard or suet
- Any dry ingredients that birds can eat, for example: unsalted peanuts, raisins, sultanas, currants, sunflower seeds, oats (not cooked), bird seed bought from a shop, hard cheese cut up small or grated.
- A mixing bowl
- A saucepan
- A wooden spoon
- A helpful grown-up

QUANTITIES:

It's best to use two thirds dry ingredients
to one third lard or suet. You can use your
yoghurt pots as a guide to how much you'll
need.

HOW TO MAKE THE FAT CAKES:

1 Ask a grown-up to melt the lard or suet
  in the saucepan, and then pour it into
  the mixing bowl.

2 Add your dry ingredients to the bowl
  and stir until it all sticks together. If
  your mixture is too runny, then add
  some more dry ingredients. If it is too
  dry and not sticking together, add some
  more melted fat.

3 Ask a grown-up to make a hole in the
  bottom of each yoghurt pot, and then
  thread the twine or string through,
  leaving a length at each end.

4 Then you can use your wooden spoon to fill the yoghurt pots with the fat cake mixture. Press the mixture down with the spoon to make them nice and firm. Make sure the string is coming up through the middle like a candle.

5 Pop them in the fridge overnight to set.

6 The next day, take them out of the fridge and pop the fat cakes out of the yoghurt pots. They should come out easily, but if not you might need a grown-up to cut the yoghurt pot with a pair of scissors.

7 Don't forget to tie a knot at one end of the string so the fat cake doesn't come off!

8 Tie the other end of the string to a tree, bush or anywhere outside where birds might come to eat.

PUFFINS ALSO 'BILL' ONE ANOTHER, WHICH IS A BIT LIKE KISSING!

How to make a paper plate puffin

Did you know that the average puffin is 25 cm high? A paper plate is 23 cm high, which means you can make a life-size puffin at home! Polly and her mummy made paper plate puffins when she was missing Neil. You can make your very own puffin, too. You could hang it from your bedroom ceiling or sit on the windowsill, imagining it flying away like Polly's puffin.

YOU WILL NEED:

- Three 23 cm wide paper plates

- Black and orange poster paint or felt tips

- A pencil and rubber

- A glue stick

- Child-friendly scissors

- A helpful grown-up

- Our templates. They can be increased in size on a photocopier or you can grade them up free-hand.

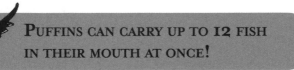

PUFFINS CAN CARRY UP TO **12** FISH IN THEIR MOUTH AT ONCE!

HOW TO MAKE A PAPER PLATE PUFFIN:

1. Use the template to draw a wing outline around the ridged rim on the back of a paper plate. Colour the edge in black with a felt tip or poster paint. If using poster paint, leave for about 60 minutes to dry. This will become the puffin's body.

2. Take a second paper plate and cut the ridged rim off, being careful with your scissors. This will become the puffin's head.

3. Use the template on the next page to pencil in a crest on top of the circle. Colour it in black, with felt tip pen or poster paint.

4. Add two black dots to make eyes in the puffin's face.

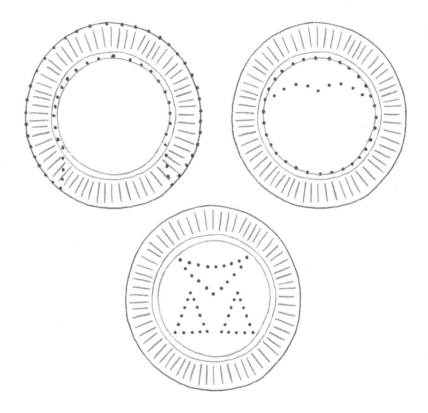

5 Once all your black paint is dry, use a glue stick to glue the bottom of the puffin's face to the top of his body. All you need now are a beak and two feet!

6 Using your third paper plate, and the templates, cut out a beak and two feet. Colour them in orange with poster paint or a felt tip. Leave to dry.

7 Use your glue stick to add the beak and feet to your puffin. You now have your very own Neil. Eep!

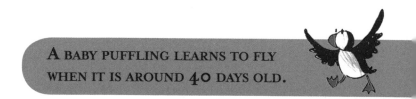

A BABY PUFFLING LEARNS TO FLY WHEN IT IS AROUND 40 DAYS OLD.

Jenny Colgan is best known for writing bestselling novels for grown-ups including *Meet Me at the Cupcake Café* and *Welcome to Rosie Hopkins' Sweetshop of Dreams*. But when a feathery character from *Little Beach Street Bakery* caught her readers' attention she knew he needed a story of his own . . .

Thomas Docherty is an acclaimed author and illustrator of children's picture books including

Little Boat, Big Scary Monster and *The Driftwood Ball*. *The Snatchabook*, which was written by his wife Helen, has been shortlisted for several awards in the UK and the US and translated into 17 languages. He loves going into schools and helping kids to write their own stories. Thomas lives in Wales by the sea with his wife and two young daughters, so he had plenty of inspiration when it came to illustrating *Polly and the Puffin*.

Neil features in Jenny's next book for grown-ups, *Summer at Little Beach Street Bakery*, as well as the next *Polly and the Puffin* book, coming in 2016.